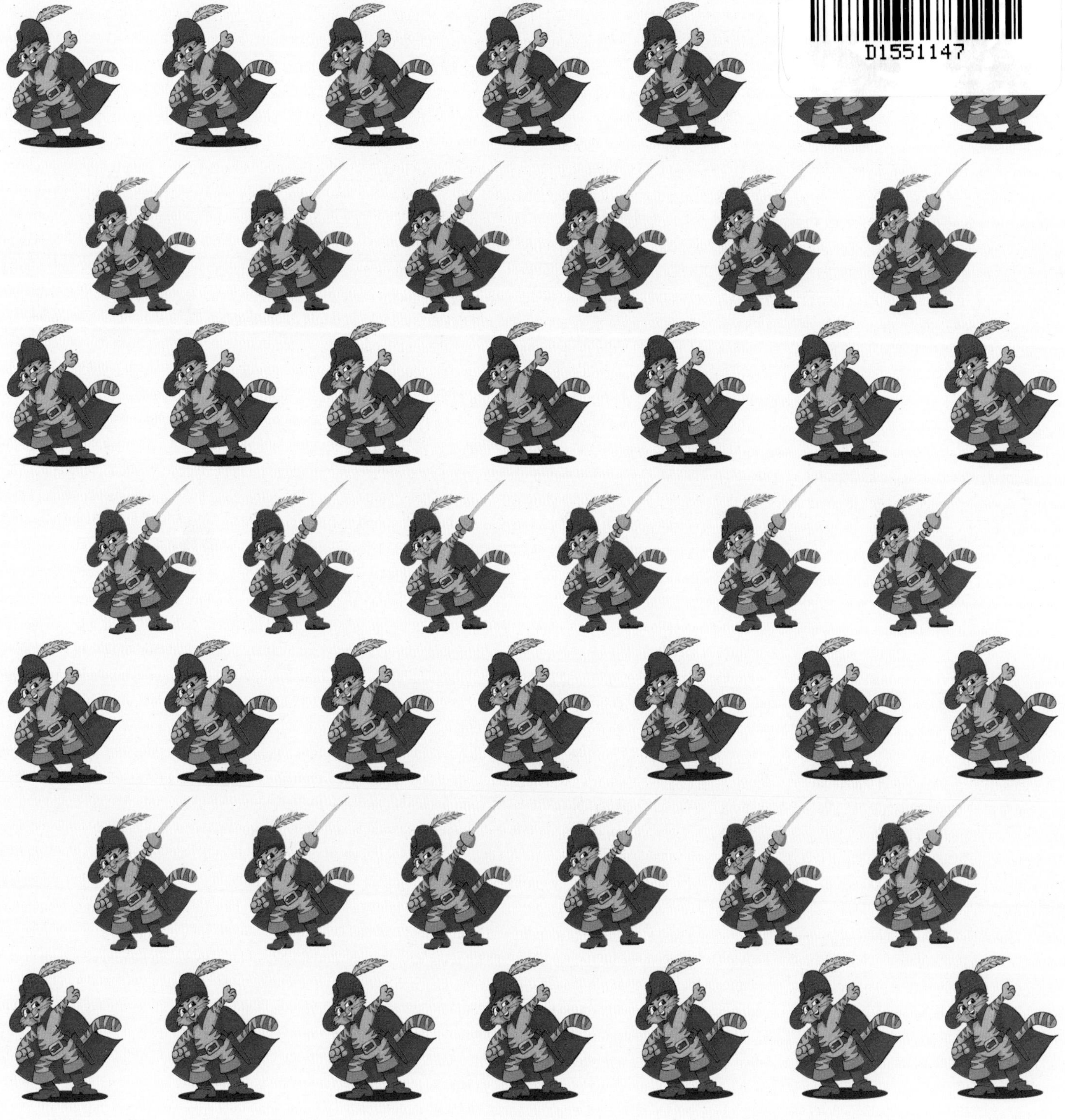

Scan the code to claim
your digital token.

THIS BOOK BELONGS TO:

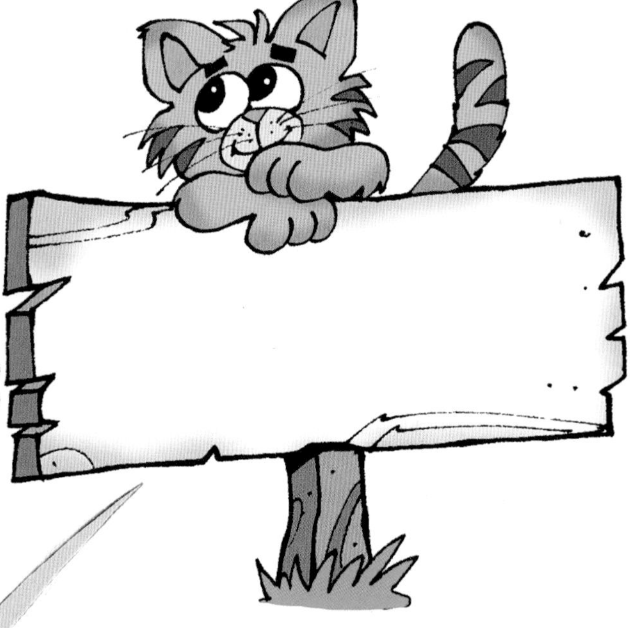

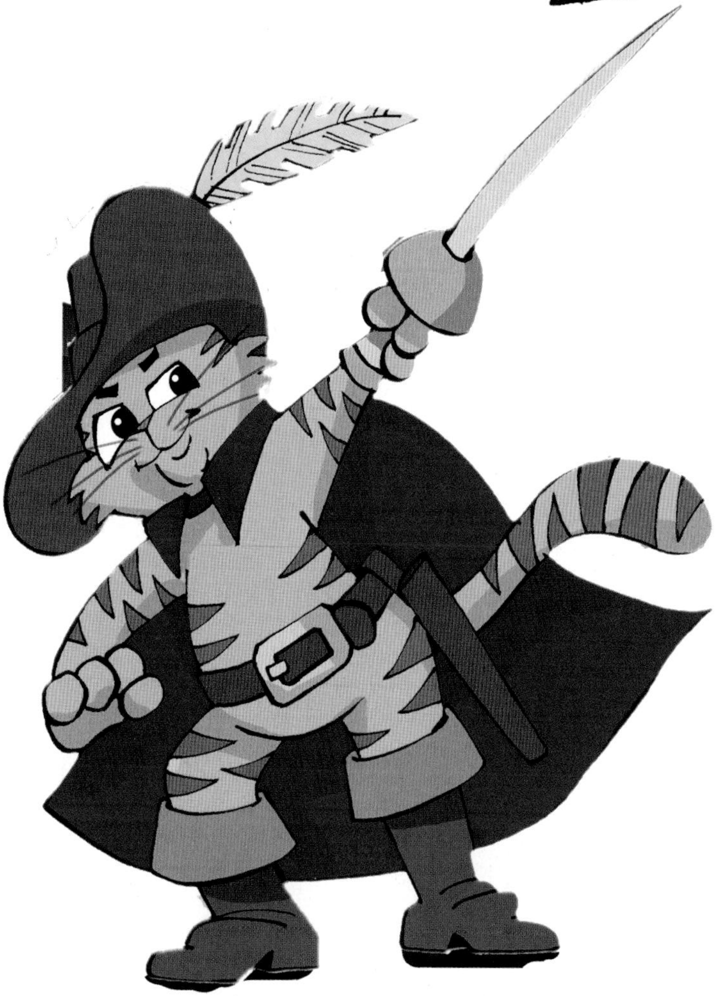

Puss in Boots

Donald Kasen and David Van Hooser

Scan this QR code with your phone camera
for more titles from imagine and wonder

Your guarantee of quality
As publishers, we strive to produce every book to the highest commercial standards.
The printing and binding have been planned to ensure a sturdy, attractive publication
which should give years of enjoyment. If your copy fails to meet our high standards,
please inform us and we will gladly replace it. admin@imagineandwonder.com

ISBN: 978-0-7396-1175-3 (Hardcover)
Library of Congress Control Number: 2021934146

Printed in China by Hung Hing Off-set Printing Co. Ltd.

Like most good adventures, this one begins once upon a time. It starts with a father who had three grownup sons. He wanted to give each of them something special, but had very little to share.

While the older sons got what little money there was, to the youngest son, Winfred, the father gave the family cat named Puss.

Feeling hopeless and sad, Winfred said to himself, "Whatever can I do with a cat?"

Just then, Puss jumped up and said, "Oh I can do many wonderful things! Just give me boots, a hat and a cape, and see what I can do!"

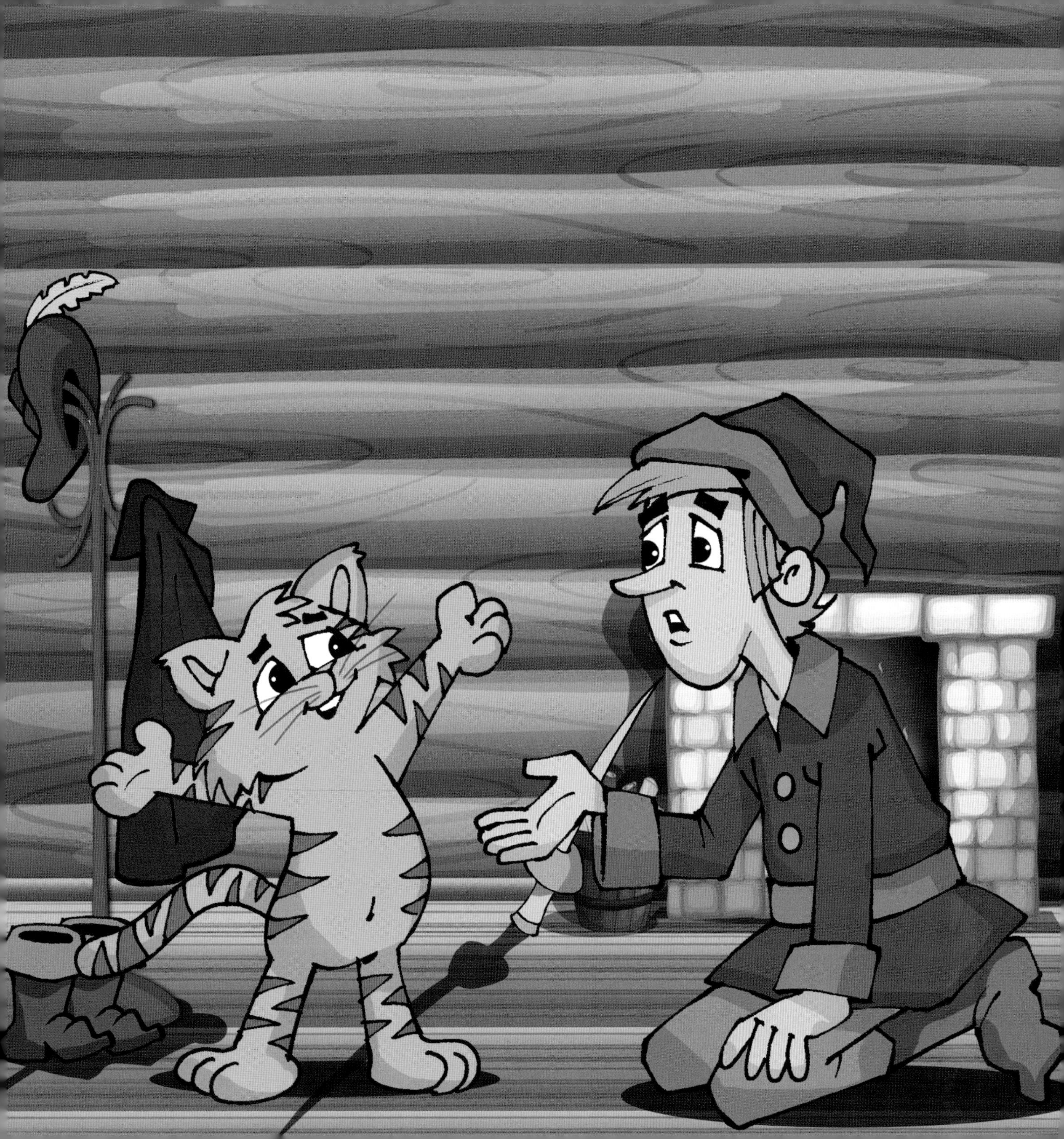

So Winfred dressed the cat in boots and clothes, and even found a tiny sword to give him. Then Puss in Boots went out into the countryside of the kingdom to see what things he could do that might bring good fortune to his young master.

In little time, Puss came to one of the King's barns filled with grain. Mice were eating it all until Puss in Boots made them stop. He forced them into an empty grain bag, then marched with the mice to the castle of the King.

"Oh mighty King," said Puss to the King. "My master, Sir Winfred, had me stop these mice from eating your grain. Now I bring them to you."

The King was pleased. "Please thank Sir Winfred for this service," he said.

The very next day, Puss in Boots walked by the King's henhouses. There, he saw two foxes stealing hens! He tied up the two thieves and again marched them to the King.

"Here, Your Majesty," Puss said. "I stopped these sly foxes from stealing your hens. My master, Sir Winfred, asked me to serve you."

"I must meet Sir Winfred some day," said the King. He gave two gold coins to Puss. "Take these to him with my thanks."

Of course, meek Winfred didn't know this was happening until Puss in Boots told him as he handed over the gold coins.

"There's nothing great or brave about me," said Winfred with a frown.

"Oh yes there is," said Puss. "But first, you must believe it."

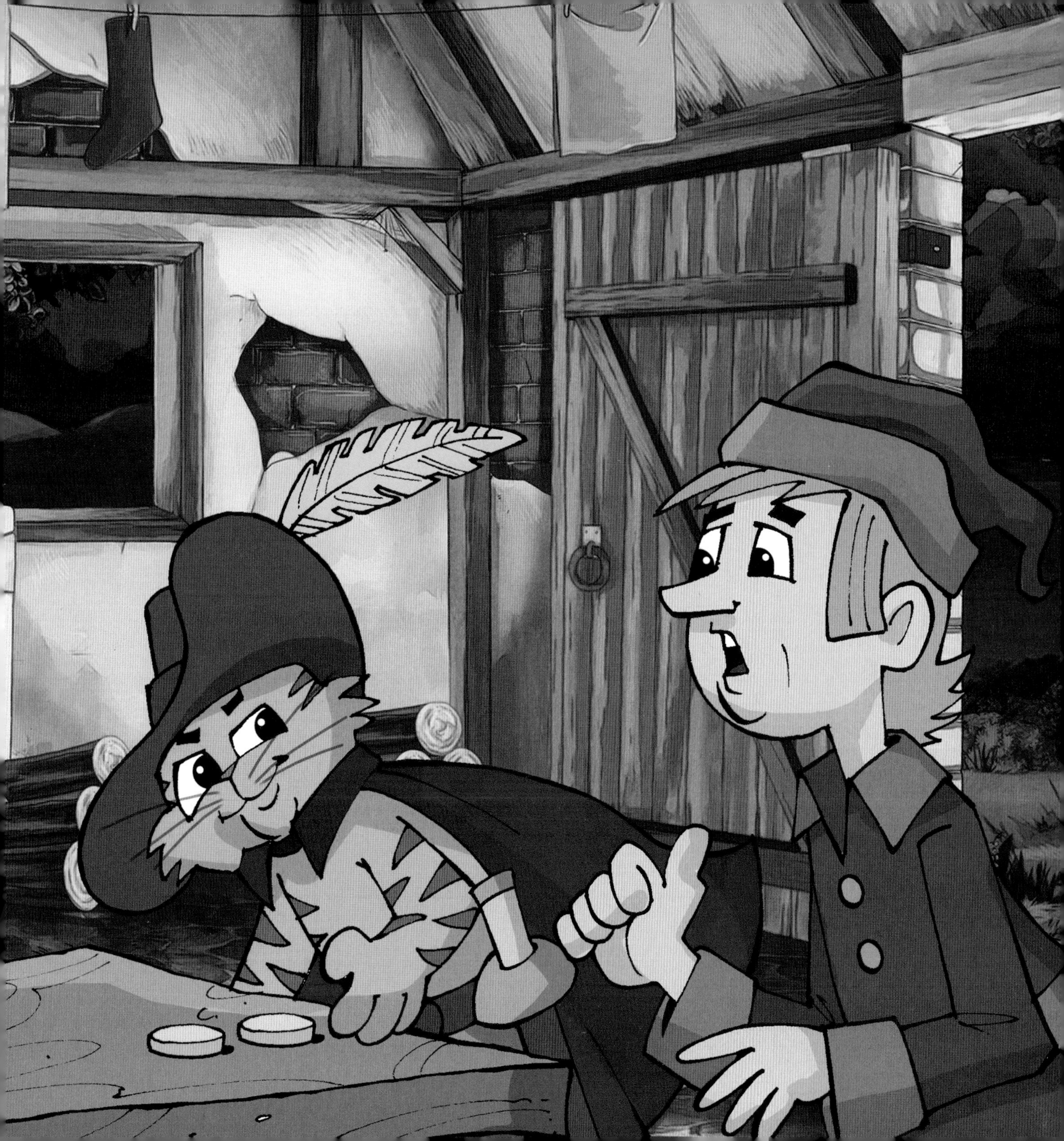

Days later, Puss in Boots was walking on the road to the King's castle. He was looking for more adventure that would help his master. Puss heard screams from a runaway carriage that was racing toward him. He stood in the road, drew his sword, and waved it at the horse!

"Halt!" said Puss. "I order you to stop!"

When the carriage stopped, Puss saw that inside it was the King's beautiful daughter, Princess Lindley.

"My driver could not control the horse," said the Princess. "Thank you, Sir Cat."

Puss bowed to her. "My master, Sir Winfred, would have me serve you any way I can. Allow me to tell you about us in song."

Later that night in the castle, Princess Lindley told her father about the noble cat. And she told him about the cat's master, Sir Winfred.

"Oh yes," said the King. "Sir Winfred has had his cat do good things for me as well. I will invite them to the castle."

Listening to this was Max, the captain of the King's guards. He and other guards planned to harm the King. Then Max would marry the Princess so the King's wealth would be his.

"We must not allow this Sir Winfred and his cat, Puss in Boots, to stop us," said Max.

When Winfred received the King's invitation, instead of being happy he was very worried.

"Once the King and his lovely daughter meet me, they will know how ugly and worthless I am! It is you who is the noble one, Puss."

"Nonsense!" replied Puss. "When they meet you tomorrow, the King and Princess will believe you are a noble prince!"

Then the clever cat took curtains, and tassels, and fancy buttons from around the house. He showed Winfred how to sew all those things into the fanciest of clothes.

Sure enough, by morning Winfred looked as royal as if he were born a prince! Before he and Puss in Boots arrived at the castle, the cat paid some traveling musicians to play music as Winfred entered the gates. Watching from the castle, the King said to the Princess, "Look! It's Sir Winfred! He even has a band to celebrate his arrival!"

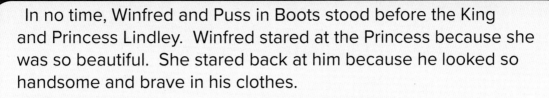

In no time, Winfred and Puss in Boots stood before the King and Princess Lindley. Winfred stared at the Princess because she was so beautiful. She stared back at him because he looked so handsome and brave in his clothes.

"Welcome, Sir Winfred," greeted the King. "I'm so glad to finally meet you."

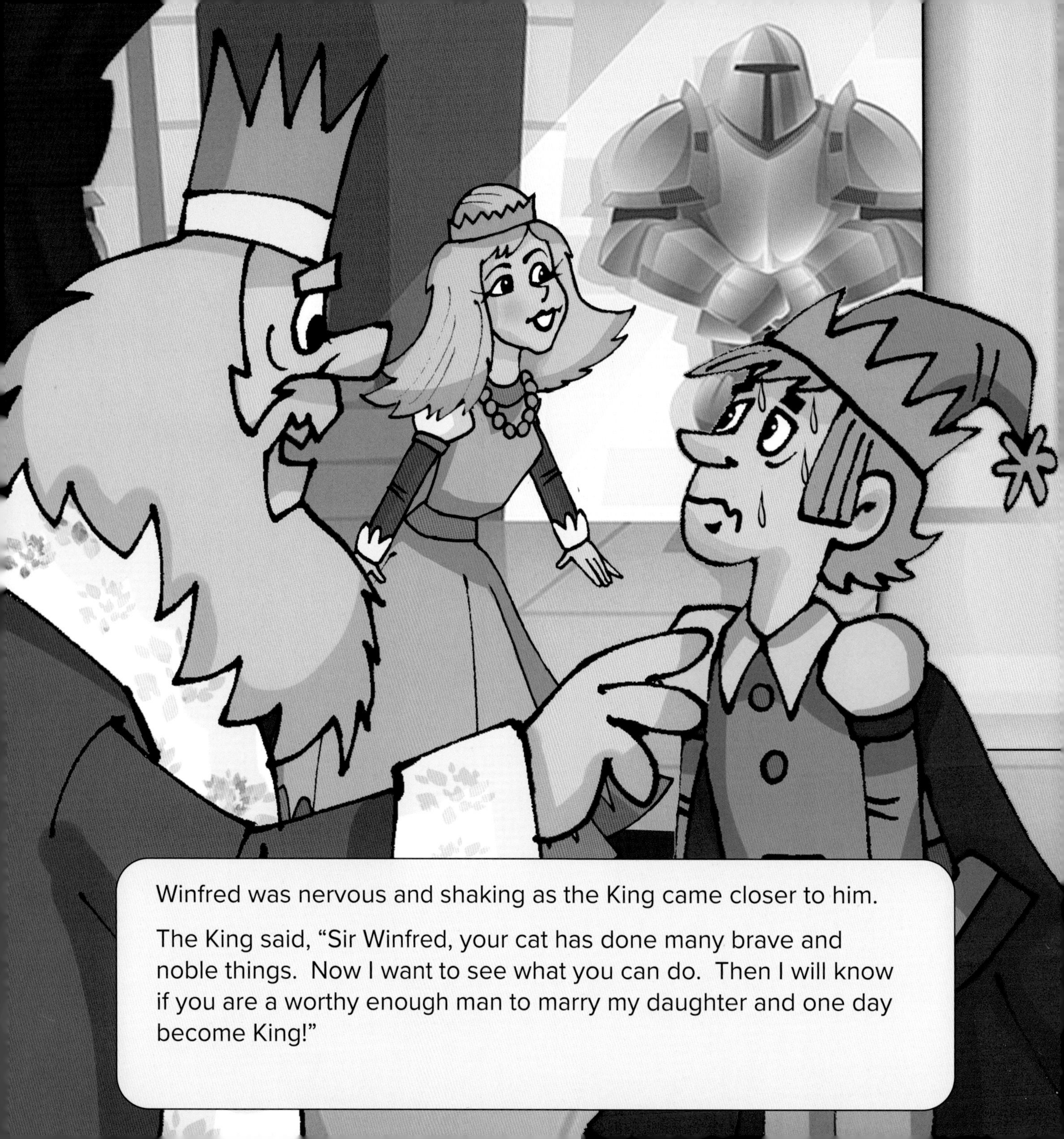

Winfred was nervous and shaking as the King came closer to him.

The King said, “Sir Winfred, your cat has done many brave and noble things. Now I want to see what you can do. Then I will know if you are a worthy enough man to marry my daughter and one day become King!”

Max, the King's evil guard, had been listening to all of this. Max knew he had to do away with the King, then stop Winfred from marrying Princess Lindley before him.

Max shouted to the other guards, "Now is the time! Attack!"

The guards drew their swords and surrounded the King and Princess. Max drew his own sword and pointed it at Winfred and Puss in Boots.

"Now, Sir Winfred, I will get rid of you and your cat!" Max said with a laugh. "Then the Princess and the kingdom will be mine!"

Winfred was too scared to move. Then Puss in Boots drew his sword and threw it to Winfred.

“Fight for the Princess!” said Puss. “You can do it! I believe in you! Now believe in yourself!”

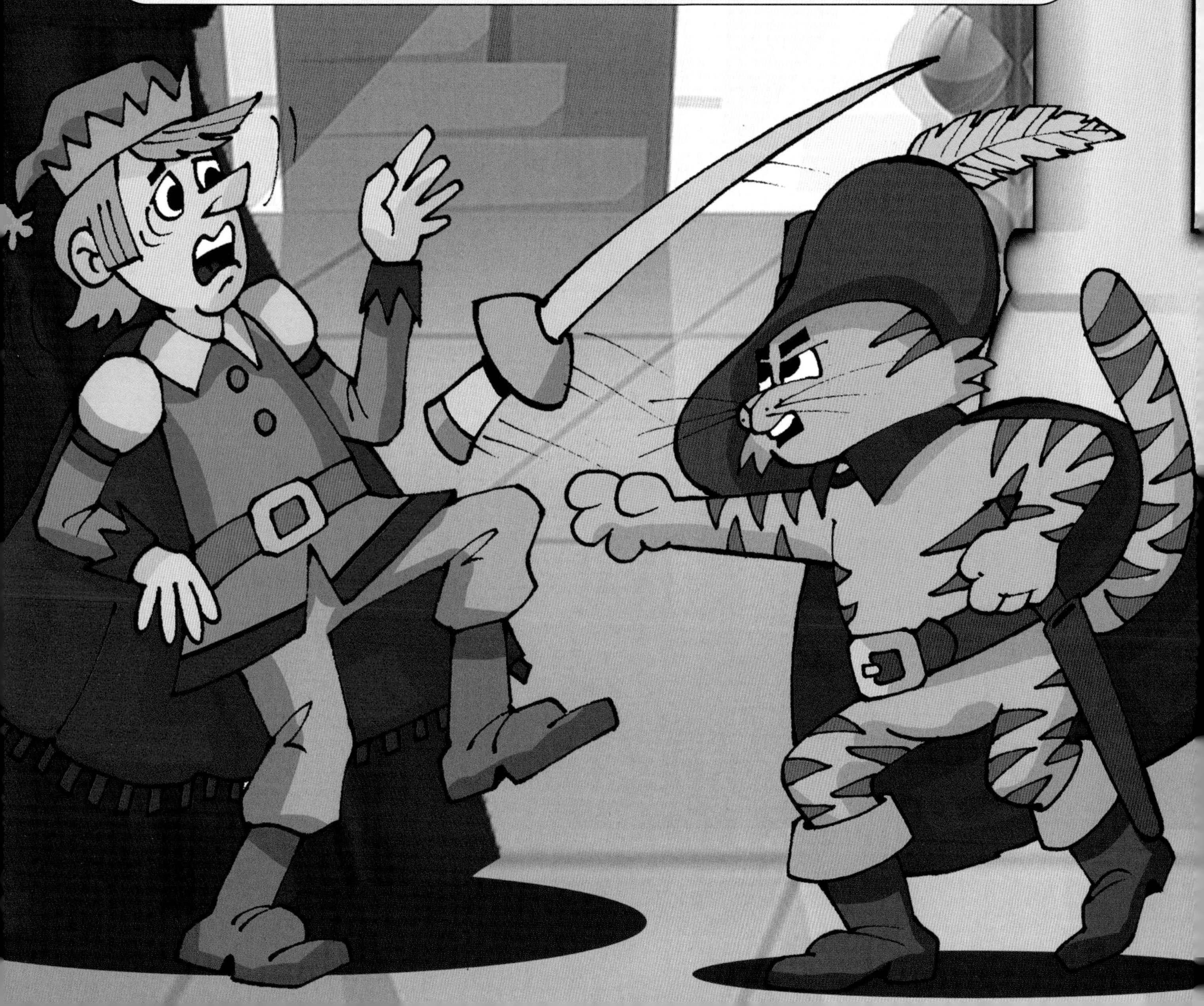

Winfred looked at the Princess, and saw how scared she was. Then Winfred started swinging his sword wildly. Max backed away from him. Puss in Boots grabbed a sword from one of the guards and jumped into the middle of them. It was the grandest sword fighting ever!

The more Winfred thought about saving Princess Lindley, the braver he got. And the more he thought about how brave he was... well, he got even braver! Winfred quickly moved back and forth. He swung his sword so fast that Max didn't know which way to run!

Puss in Boots pulled a rug which made the guards fall and drop their swords. Winfred backed Max against a wall. The evil guard was so scared, he threw down his sword.

“Enough! I give up!” shouted Max.

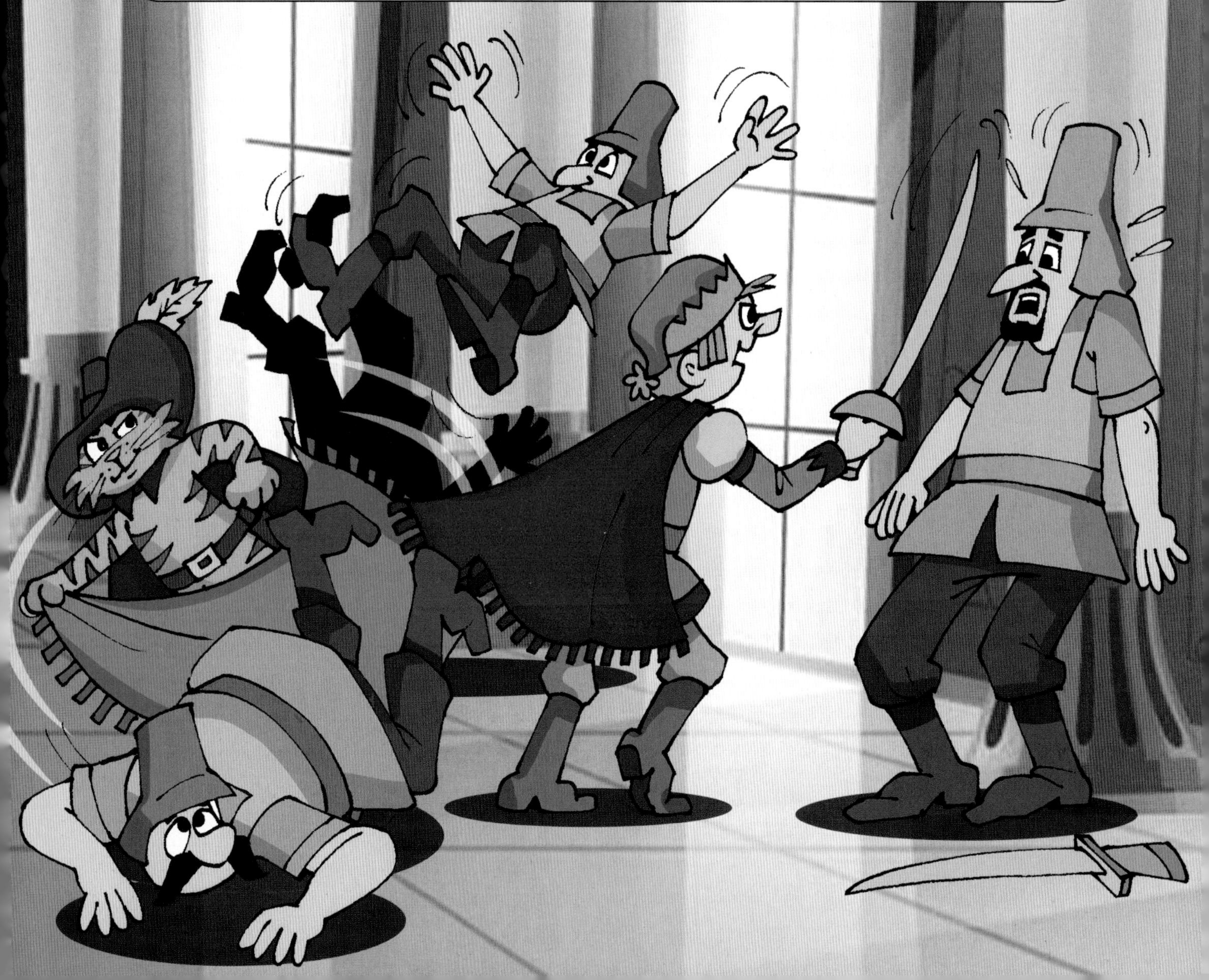

The King called in his loyal soldiers. They took Max and the other guards away. Princess Lindley ran into Winfred's arms.

"Sir Winfred, you have saved us," said the King. "You are indeed a brave and good man! You shall marry my daughter. And I will make Puss in Boots the captain of my guards!"

Puss in Boots looked to Winfred and smiled.

"You see," said the noble cat. "A brave and strong person was inside you all this time! I am proud of you."

Then Winfred replied, "And I am proud of you, Puss in Boots!"

COLLECT THE SET FROM PETER PAN PRESS

Scan the code to see these titles
and more on www.ImagineAndWonder.com

Peter Pan PRESS

COMING SOON

THE
RAVEN

the
Tell-Tale Heart

THE LEGEND OF
SLEEPY
HOLLOW

Opposites
Short and Tall ... and That's Not All
Donald Kasen and David Van Hooser
Illustrated by Rick Incrocci

CHILDREN'S ALL-TIME FAVORITE BIBLE STORIES
Jesus Is Born
Jesus Is Born and 17 More All-time Favorite Bible Stories from the New Testament
Peter Pan
V. Gilbert Beers and Ronald A. Beers

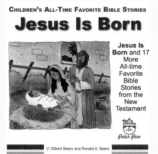

Scan the QR code to find other
amazing adventures and more from
www.ImagineAndWonder.com

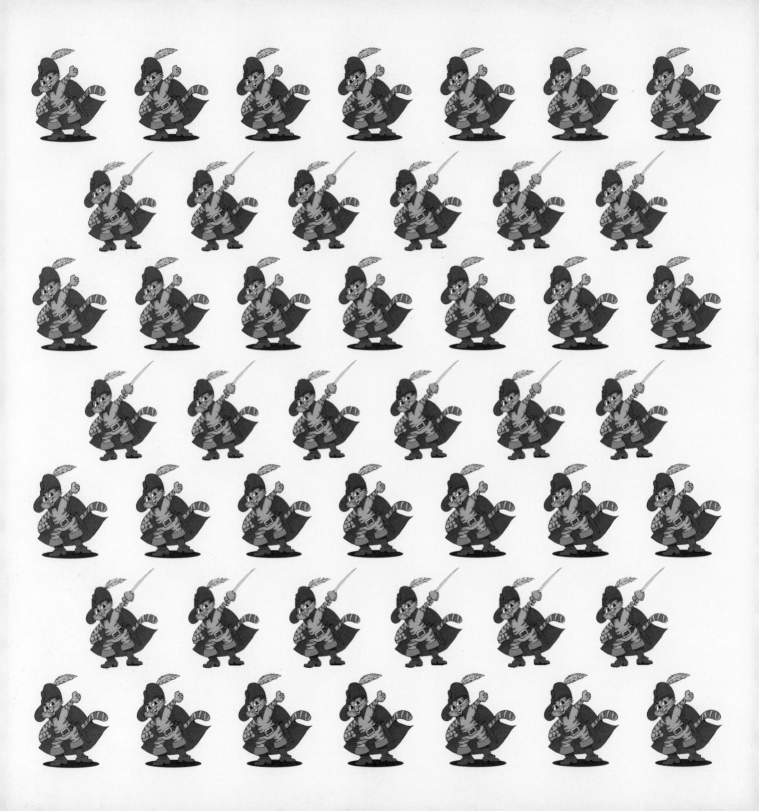